# Giovanni's Light

The Story of a Town Where
Time Stopped for Christmas

## Phyllis Theroux

SCRIBNER

SCRIBNER
1230 Avenue of the Americas
New York, NY 10020

SCRIBNER and design are trademarks of
Macmillan Library Reference USA, Inc., used under license by
Simon & Schuster, the publisher of this work.

For information regarding special discounts for bulk purchases,
please contact Simon & Schuster Special Sales at 1-800-456-6798 or
*business@simonandschuster.com*

*Designed by Kyoko Watanabe*

Set in Garamond 3

Manufactured in the United States of America

1 3 5 7 9 10 8 6 4 2

Library of Congress Cataloging-in-Publication Data is available.

ISBN 0-7432-4433-8

*For Ashland,*
*with love*

*Giovanni's Light*

# *Chapter One*

RYLAND FALLS, population thirty-five hundred, was a town that didn't look quite real. With its quiet, tree-shaded streets, old-fashioned clapboard houses with wraparound porches, and lawns thick with fireflies on summer evenings, it made people sigh and imagine happy things that had never happened to them. There were vacant lots full of buttercups and Queen Anne's lace, a creek with frogs and large, flat stones for sitting. Children rode their bicycles downtown for ice cream. Everybody knew everybody else's name.

City people called Ryland Falls a backwater, and it's true that not a lot happened here from one year to the next. But in spring, the pear trees along Center Street sent drifts of white petals into air that smelled of fresh grass clippings. In summer, willows formed a soft green drizzle of branches around the pond. And when the air grew cold, the maples on top of Cemetery Hill burst into flame and burned for long blue days before dropping their leaves like a bright tablecloth upon the graves.

In the distance was a mountain. Old Rag was as wild and trackless as Ryland Falls was orderly and refined, and the townspeople didn't spend much time there, except on the road that cut across the top of it. But it gave the town a picturesque backdrop and protected it from the noise and confusion of the big city on the other side.

Ryland Falls had its share of sad people, lonely people, and impatient people, like Miranda Bridgeman, who thought it was the dullest place on earth, and she couldn't wait until she was old enough to leave. Every house had its own private cup of sorrow, although some were fuller than others, and no mountain was large enough to keep out the demands of time.

The demands had built up slowly, over many years, so that nobody really noticed how much faster the pace of life had become. But a town that looked sleepy was, in fact, full of people who had to wake up earlier and earlier to keep up with their own lives.

By 6:15 A.M., half the newspapers were already snatched up off the sidewalks. By 6:45, Reverend Williams was on his second cup of coffee and going over his day's calendar, which usually had three hospital visits and a meeting before lunchtime. And by 7:15, the school bus was rumbling down Center Street, full of children still brushing toast crumbs off their lips, on the way to school.

Like every other place on earth, Ryland Falls was full of busy people who had too much to do. But that was the price of modern life and nobody complained.

Then, too, living in Ryland Falls made the faster pace easy to ignore. The librarian automatically renewed your overdue books, the postman would add a stamp from his own pocket if there wasn't enough postage on a letter, and if somebody left the car lights on by mistake, somebody else would knock on the front door with the news.

Ryland Falls wasn't paradise, but it didn't take long for newcomers to realize that most people went out of their way to be kind. And there was a certain golden quality about the town—the way the light dusted the shop windows, threaded its way down back alleys, and lit up a stand of daylilies stretching their necks like trumpets toward the sun—that made visitors catch their breath and say, "Oh, my goodness! I didn't know that places like this existed except in storybooks!"

As in a book, the order of the stories never changed. On December 1, the Chamber of Commerce always hung out the "Yuletide Greetings" banners from all the downtown lampposts. The inflatable plastic Santa Claus went back on top of the firehouse roof, and grumpy Diane started wearing her set of imitation rein-deer antlers behind the counter at Elwood's Market.

"Happy holidays," she would say glumly as she handed a customer change. "My brother died last month."

"Oh, I'm sorry to hear that."

"Thanks, and my aunt died the month before that."

"Goodness, you've been having quite a time. I hope you feel better soon."

"I'm trying but I was up half the night coughing."

Grumpy Diane could be counted on to come up with these kinds of sinking remarks, but most people let them roll right off the counter. They knew what to expect, which was one of the reasons why Ryland Falls was such a pleasant place to live. You knew what to expect from everything. Even Christmas.

The gingerbread-house contest was always announced right after Thanksgiving. Next, the tickets for the house tour and Christmas tea went on sale. Then came the annual *Messiah* community sing-along. On Christmas Eve, people gathered in front of All Saints Church while the children chosen to be in the

"Living Nativity" scene shivered for a holy cause in a plywood manger. And on Christmas night, almost everybody—with one sad and glaring exception—took their children to Cemetery Hill for a town sledding party.

Almost everything that happened in Ryland Falls was a repetition of something that had taken place last year, or a hundred years ago. That was part of its charm.

But on this particular Christmas, there were signs that the usual order of things was going to be disturbed. They weren't very large signs, at least not in the beginning. But even if they had been, most of the people in Ryland Falls would have been too busy with their own lives to notice.

# Chapter Two

ON THE MORNING of December 1, Ryland Falls lay nestled like a toy village at the foot of Old Rag Mountain. A hard coat of frost covered all the streets and gardens. Fish hung motionless beneath a lid of ice upon the pond. Trees that in the summertime were thick with leaves thrust their bare arms into the winter sky and froze against it. Nothing moved, including the towns-people, who were still dreaming deep beneath their quilts and blankets—except for Neddie Crimmins.

On the third floor, in a large, toy-filled room in the biggest house in Ryland Falls, eight-year-old Neddie was wide-awake and staring at the ceiling above his bed. He was trying to imagine the expression on his father's face, but he couldn't get it quite right. Shock? Astonishment? He blinked his eyes and stared some more.

Neddie's father, Edward Benchley Crimmins, had made his fortune in clocks—all different kinds of clocks—and the Crimmins Clock Tower at the foot of Center Street was the town's tallest and most impres-sive monument. Every hour on the hour it reminded people in solemn, deep-throated tones of two things—that time was a serious matter and that Edward Crim-mins had made the most of it.

Edward Crimmins was rarely home. With factories around the world, he spent most of his time traveling between them. Today, however, was an exception. He was not only home, but in a stroke of luck that didn't usually come Neddie's way, he was coming to Open House at Neddie's school. Neddie had a surprise for him. One of his drawings, of a chair that could fly, had won the school's first prize.

Neddie was a dreamer who liked to imagine things he had never seen: jet-propelled sleds, portable wings, and magic carpets that could whisk him around the world, like his father's private jet, in the blink of an eye. This habit of dreaminess worried Edward Crimmins, who saw it as a lack of focus that would make it harder for Neddie to succeed in later life.

"He's got to branch out a little," he told Neddie's mother, "take some interest in a few more activities. What about soccer?"

Olivia Crimmins sighed. "He hates soccer."

"Well, then, *something!* Maybe next summer he could go to a computer camp. Or get into a Scouting program."

Edward Crimmins wanted Neddie to be more of a regular boy and didn't think that bending over an art tablet drawing magic carpets was the way.

Last night, he had stuck his head into Neddie's

room at bedtime and found him sitting cross-legged on his bed with a pad of paper across his knees.

"Mind if I have a look?" he asked.

Neddie handed him a half-finished drawing of a dragon.

"As dragons go, I'd say it's a pretty good likeness. Is it part of a school project?"

"No," said Neddie. "I'm just practicing. Mr. Campbell said artists have to keep practicing."

Edward Crimmins handed the drawing back. "In a perfect world, Neddie, I'd say keep on with it. But I have to tell you, there's no real future in being an artist, unless you've got somebody else to pay the bills."

Neddie's face fell.

Edward Crimmins loved his son and didn't want to hurt his feelings so he tried to soften the truth a little. Laying his hand on Neddie's shoulder he used a gentler voice.

"I don't have anything against art, Neddie. Lord knows we need our van Goghs and Michelangelos. And you've got some talent. No question about it. But someday you'll be a grown man, with all the responsibilities that come along with age, and now's the only time you've got to prepare for the rest of your life."

Edward Crimmins looked around his son's room. The shelves were filled with books, toys, and board games. A collection of handmade silk kites was suspended from the ceiling. Circus posters hung on the walls. And everywhere—dangling off the window seat, clumped together on a chair, or surrounding him on his bed—was Neddie's ragtag army of stuffed animals. It was the privileged sanctuary of a child who lived more in his imagination than in the real world, and Edward Crimmins didn't know how to bridge the gap. He decided to take a different tack.

"There are other ways to use your talent, Neddie, and still be pointed in the direction you want to go. You can use computers to draw, just like you're doing with a pen, only better. Computers are the big excitement now, and it's where you need to spend your time—to *save* time."

Neddie's father was always talking about saving time, as if it were a ball of string and the more you had the more you could tie things up with it.

"Why, do you know," he continued, "you can look up anything on the Web—"

"I know that, Dad," said Neddie, interrupting.

"—like ink gel pens, and—whomp!—up comes five hundred places on the screen where you can find them—just like that!"

Neddie stared down at the ink gel pen in his hand. "But I already have some," he said quietly.

Edward Crimmins sighed, his patience almost gone. "You're missing my point, Son. It's not about pens, it's about computers helping kids to stay on top of things . . . so down the road, in the future, you can get a good job, like mine, Neddie boy!"

This was how the conversation always ended between Neddie and his father—with Neddie's future, as if that were all that mattered. But the furthest Neddie could think was the Open House tonight. He refocused his eyes upon the ceiling and imagined his father standing in front of his drawing.

"What!" Edward Crimmins would exclaim when he saw the bright blue satin ribbon hanging next to it. He would push his glasses up the bridge of his nose, the way he did whenever he got excited, and say, "Neddie my boy, how long has this been going on— under my own roof?" No, first he would whisper into Neddie's mother's ear, "I'm floored, Olivia. I'm floored." That was one of his favorite expressions.

Then, and this was the part that filled Neddie's rib cage with butterflies, he would wrap his arm around Neddie's shoulder, pull him to his side, and say to Neddie's art teacher in a loud, proud voice that everyone could hear, "Tell me, Mr. Campbell, how is it possible that someone who is only eight years old could be producing work that is so advanced?"

Edward Benchley Crimmins had no time for art. But today was the day that Neddie Crimmins was going to change his mind.

His imagination drifted down the wide, polished stairs and into his parents' bedroom, where they were still asleep. When his father was home, it was like finding the last piece in the puzzle. When you pressed the last piece into the middle of the picture, all the other pieces fit tightly against each other.

Downtown, the clock tower struck the hour. Neddie counted the chimes. It was only 5 A.M. Sitting up in bed, he looked out the window. Everything outside was moon-colored, except for Old Rag, whose flanks were dark against the sky. Suddenly a pinprick of light flashed halfway up the mountain. Someone else was awake, too.

# Chapter Three

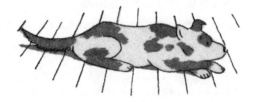

GIOVANNI WOKE UP and rubbed his beard, which is what he did when he wanted to remember something. Pushing Max like a warm quilt to the foot of the bed, he dressed quickly and walked into the kitchen. It was still dark out, but through the window he could see that the ground was still bare. How strange, he thought. There was always snow on the mountain by

December 1. But this year, even though the creek had frozen and the woods were full of frost ferns, the snow had not come.

He lit a lantern and set it on the widow ledge next to his portable radio. He would need to take that with him. The alarm clicked on. "Goood morning," sang out the announcer, "it's five A.M. and going to be another cold one. The temperature . . ."

Giovanni reached up and turned the radio off. Everything he needed to know about the temperature, he could see in his own breath.

He fed a log into the woodstove to warm up the room and began to fill up an empty box upon the table with supplies. Max's head pressed against his knee and Giovanni looked down at him and smiled.

"You don't want me to forget to put something in for you, do you?"

Reaching down beneath the table, he took an almost empty sack of dog biscuits and tossed it into the box. More dog food for Max was on his mental list of things he needed to buy in town.

Giovanni was the last remaining member of a

mountain family that had lived on Old Rag as long as anybody could remember. They were blacksmiths, roofers, handymen, and housecleaners—people who left school early and slipped in and out of Ryland Falls to earn a living but always returned to the mountain by nightfall. Giovanni's cabin sat upon land that had been passed down from one generation to another until, finally, no one else was left to inherit it. One by one, they had died or been softened by thoughts of civilization and left.

It was a hard but independent life. There was no electricity, no running water, and no heat or cooking range except for the woodstove. But there was a well behind the house, and a vegetable garden provided Giovanni with most of the food he ate. And whenever he needed something he couldn't make himself, he paid a visit to Ryland Falls' town dump. It always amazed him what people threw away.

Once he'd found an old front door and a barbershop chair that he'd turned into a table he could pump up and down with his foot. The goggle-shaped window above the sink had been a windshield. Most of the tools hanging in the makeshift forge behind the cabin had come from salvaged car parts of high-quality steel thrown out by auto dealers after a recall. But the best, most high-quality thing he had ever found at the town dump was Max.

He had been barely a month old when Giovanni had seen him walking unsteadily toward him over a pile of rubbish—a trembling, pitiful-looking puppy with stick-out ribs and sad, licorice-colored eyes. Giovanni was shy around people. But there wasn't a fox, deer, or jackrabbit within a mile of his cabin that he didn't speak to as if it were an old friend. When he saw Max, he knew just what to do. He stood still and waited.

When Max reached Giovanni's side, he was too weak to do anything more than lean against his legs, exhausted. Kneeling down to pat his head, Giovanni examined his rough, tricolor coat. He was probably a German shepherd–retriever mix.

"Hey, little fella," he murmured. "Where's your collar? How'd you get here?" But Giovanni knew the answer to that one. Somebody had abandoned Max at the dump as carelessly as an old suitcase.

Giovanni had been alone for a long time. Though Lucia had died twenty years ago, he could still see her sitting on the porch steps, balancing little Carlo on her knee while she shelled peas for supper. It had been ten years since Carlo had left to join the army, and seven since a pale young officer about Carlo's age had mounted the same porch steps and knocked upon the door to tell Giovanni that his son was dead.

Giovanni had grown too old and taciturn to want to be anybody's husband now. And the rage and grief he had felt over Carlo's death—so senseless that for years he couldn't think about it without feeling sharp pains in his heart—had finally turned into resignation, the resignation into calm. Sorrow had hollowed out Giovanni like a gourd, and the emptiness inside was not unpleasant. But the way Max leaned against his legs like a last resort turned his mind in a new direction.

Well, Giovanni thought, perhaps it's meant to be. Gently gathering up the puppy in one hand, he unbuttoned his jacket with the other and slipped him inside. Max gave a little shudder and lay quietly against Giovanni's chest. "Never mind," he said, patting Max through his jacket like a baby in a blanket, "you're home now."

From that day on, Max had been Giovanni's constant companion, running just ahead of him as he gathered wood, picked berries, and planted tree seedlings. Giovanni knew how to live off the land better than anyone else around. But some things, such as coffee, kerosene, and the occasional dog biscuit for Max, required money. For that, Giovanni had his Christmas trees.

Growing Christmas trees suited Giovanni's solitary, observant nature. The ground beneath the trees had to be kept constantly cropped to prevent diseases. In the spring and fall, he trimmed up the branches so they would grow into the graceful shapes that people in Ryland Falls wanted. Then, as winter approached, he would walk between fragrant rows of Scotch pine, blue spruce, and Douglas fir and tie ribbons around the ones that were mature enough to cut down.

All last week, Giovanni had worked well into the night cutting, hauling, and loading the trees upon his truck. His back ached and his mind rebelled against the trip that lay ahead, but it was time to go. Picking up the box of provisions, he stepped outside onto the porch and drew a deep breath as if to take the mountain with him in his lungs. Locking the door, he called to Max, "Come on, boy, we're ready."

In truth, Giovanni was never ready to leave the mountain. He loved everything about it—how the birds formed a wreath of song around the roof in the early morning, the sound of the melting creek tumbling over the rocks in the spring, the way the wind bent the treetops during a storm. The face of Old Rag was constantly changing its expressions, and Giovanni hated to miss any one of them. But three weeks of camping out in Ryland Falls made it possible for him to live on the mountain the rest of the year.

Walking toward the truck, he mentally ticked off everything that should be loaded on it: army tent, portable woodstove, firewood, cot, bedding. All there. Radio. Yes. Then he remembered something he had left behind. Letting himself back into the cabin, he walked over to his bed and picked up a large, tattered book on the bedside table and tucked it under his arm. He never left it behind. Climbing back into the truck, he put the engine in gear and headed down the mountain.

When Giovanni reached Ryland Falls, the Crimmins Clock Tower had just chimed six o'clock. He drove past the inn, the police station, the library, and several blocks of stores—the Whistle Stop Ice Cream Parlour, Workout Wonder Gym, Shear Power Hair Salon, First National Bank. It was always a shock to Giovanni when he returned to civilization.

On the mountain, Giovanni's days were regulated by heat and cold, light and darkness. Off the mountain, these things were taken care of, and the standards of measurement were full and empty, fast and slow. Giovanni gripped the wheel and stared straight ahead. At the far end of Center Street was Elwood's Market. Next to Elwood's was a vacant lot where every year Giovanni sold his trees.

He pulled to a stop. Max jumped out of the truck, did a brief patrol of the lot, then followed Giovanni as he set up camp with a woodsman's efficiency. First he erected the army tent. Next, he put together the woodstove and fit the stovepipe through a flap in the center of the canvas roof. Then he got a fire going and arranged his cot and provisions along the walls. Outside, it was below freezing, but soon the inside of his tent was as warm and cozy as his mountain cabin.

Then Giovanni unloaded his trees, their branches rustling like silk as he pulled them off the truck. Nobody could ask for trees that were fresher or more gracefully shaped, and as he arranged them all by height and kind in orderly rows upon the lot, he began to cheer up. The smell of pine sap, mingled with the wood smoke from his stove, made him feel as if he were back on the mountain.

By seven-thirty, everything was in place. Pulling a wooden chair across the entrance of the tent so the stove would warm his back, he sat down to rest and survey the small mock forest in front of him. Max laid his head upon his knee and looked up at him reproachfully. Giovanni smiled.

"You want to go home, too, don't you? Well, we'll be back by Christmas . . . maybe sooner."

Giovanni cast his eyes toward the sky and tried to

decide whether it had the look of snow. A little snow on the branches always made his trees sell better. But he wasn't worried. Every one of them was a beauty and Giovanni knew he would sell them all.

Meanwhile, in a second-floor apartment above Elwood's Market, a tall young man with rumpled hair stood at the window and looked down at the man and the dog. His pale, appraising eyes took in the whole scene: the woodsman in his rough coat, the light cast by the open stove door upon the inside of the tent, the gentle line of the dog's mouth as he rested his head upon the woodsman's knee. Will Campbell was a painter. Automatically, he noticed these kinds of details and put a frame around them. But the scene did not inspire him to paint. He shivered. He had promised himself that he would come to a decision by Christmas, and Giovanni's trees reminded him that Christmas was almost here.

# *Chapter Four*

FROM THE MOMENT he'd stepped off the bus in front of Elwood's Market, Will Campbell had made a distinct impression. A black duffel bag was slung over one shoulder. Tucked beneath his arm was a skateboard, also black, but with hand-painted silver edges. He fished inside his pocket for a piece of paper. The school was at the other end of Center Street. Stuffing the directions back into his pocket, he slapped down his skateboard, stepped on, and pushed off. Riding down the middle of town on a skateboard, he looked like a tree on wheels, and long after people in Ryland Falls had grown accustomed to the sight, they still held their breath when they saw him coming. The children thought he had suction cups on the bottom of his shoes. But Will Campbell had something better. He had grace.

Will never raised his voice when he spoke to his students. With the smaller children, he knelt down so they wouldn't have to crane their neck to see him. His eyes were sharp but kind, and it seemed to amuse him to see children misbehave when he knew that deep down they didn't really want to misbehave, but were just feeling lonely or misunderstood or wanted to go outside and play instead of sitting in a hot classroom. All he had to do was point a finger or look in a particular direction and the entire class would follow his eyes, like members of a symphony orchestra.

Will Campbell had a magic hold on the children,

and at times the principal wondered what exactly Will did to keep their attention without seeming to exert the least bit of authority over them. Peering through the window into Will's classroom, he would see him sitting, like a disjointed scarecrow in his all-black outfit, with crossed legs on a stool, talking to them or holding up a student's work.

Fortunately, thought the principal, Will Campbell was only part-time. Too many free spirits in one school could undermine the whole operation. Still the principal had to admit that the school had never had a more gifted art instructor. Children who used to have trouble holding a crayon were now producing nice work. Too bad, he thought, it was in the wrong subject. If only he could find as gifted teachers for the math and science departments, that would really put the school on the map.

※

Will turned away from the window, plucked his jacket off the bedpost, and headed for the door. Tonight was Open House at school and he had to get there extra early to hang his students' work. Grabbing his skate-board, he fumbled his way down the narrow wooden staircase, walked through the meat department, and into the darkened market.

It was seven-thirty and Elwood's Market didn't open for another half an hour, but Tommy Elwood was standing inside the front window, trying to untangle a bunch of Christmas lights.

"Looks like you've got your hands full," said Will.

Tommy nodded. "They never put them away right. Every year it's the same thing."

Outside, Will stepped onto his skateboard and shoved off from the curb. Behind him, lying in a messy stack on the floor of his apartment, was a pile of half-finished drawings in various stages of development. None of them came close to what he had intended, and one by one he had shoved them aside. As he pushed himself down the street to school, Will felt that he was leaving one scene of failure and heading toward another.

Only a year ago when he had first arrived in Ryland Falls, fresh out of art school and dreaming of becoming a great artist, all he had needed was a part-time job that would pay the bills. The ad on the school's job-placement bulletin board sounded perfect—"Wanted: part-time art teacher in Ryland Falls Elementary School. Drive bus as needed."

The pay was low and the only place he could afford to rent was the storage room and bath above Elwood's Market. But his needs had been few, the light was good, and after he had pushed all the tin buckets, busted chairs, and old toothpaste display racks into a corner, plenty of room was left over for a bed and work-space. He was twenty-three and eager to begin his life. Now, at twenty-four, he was beginning to think the price of living in Ryland Falls was too high.

He taught children whose parents didn't really believe in art. They were quick to tell him how much the children loved him and how important art was—oh, very important! But the school board only gave out serious money for the math and science departments, and this year, it had voted to do away with recess in kindergarten—so the children could spend more time in the computer lab.

For another thing, part-time didn't mean half-time. It meant interrupted time, with so many demands to go to meetings and fill out forms that Will was usually too tired at the end of the day to paint anything for himself. Yesterday, he had come home and tried to do a simple sketch of a bowl of grapes on a stool. But he had fallen asleep with the pencil in his hand.

Will had not lost his eye for beauty. He could still see it, just as plainly as he could see Old Rag Mountain. But less and less was he moved to do anything about it. His heart for art was weakening. Weary, disappointed, and beginning to wonder whether he really had the drive he needed to persevere, Will could feel the fire inside him going out. He couldn't let that happen.

Gliding to a stop in front of the school, he kicked his skateboard up and under his arm—a deft one-two motion that every child tried to imitate without success. Whenever Will Campbell thought about leaving Ryland Falls, the children made him hesitate.

Ryland Falls was full of decent, hardworking people who loved their children and wanted what was best for them. But most of them believed only what they could see right in front of them, like a well-mowed lawn or a good report card. Children like Neddie Crimmins—and there were more of them than their own parents knew—wanted to see what wasn't there, except in their imaginations. If he left, who would be there to protect them, to tell them that staring out the window was an important part of keeping their imaginations strong?

He unlocked the art room and went to his desk, which was piled high with students' work to hang on the walls. Neddie Crimmins's drawing was on top. Will looked down at it and smiled. "The Best Chair in the World" was eccentric, whimsical, and accurate, just like Neddie. Picking up the drawing, he walked out into the hall and looked for the best spot. Yes. He would hang it right outside the principal's office, so Neddie's father couldn't miss it.

# Chapter Five

EDWARD BENCHLEY CRIMMINS took a watch out of his vest pocket and laid it on the breakfast table. Arranged in a neat fan by his napkin were a half dozen travel brochures. On Christmas Day, Neddie and his parents always flew out of town to a warm, sunny place for their annual Christmas vacation.

Shaking the napkin into his lap, he scanned the brochure covers and the note his wife had clipped on top of them. ("December 1st is the reservation deadline. We have to decide today.")

"I don't have time to go through these this morning, Olivia. I've got a meeting in half an hour. What do you recommend?"

Olivia Crimmins cast a sidelong glance at Neddie, whose face was hidden behind a cereal box. She knew he was scowling. That morning, when he'd come down for breakfast, he'd seen the brochures and dropped like a rock into his chair. "Why can't we be like everybody else and just stay home and open presents!"

"Your father," she'd replied, "needs the vacation. And so do I, for that matter. And Christmas is the one time of year that we can all be together and just be a family—with no interruptions."

Neddie had stared glumly at his place mat. "Everybody else gets to go sledding on Cemetery Hill on Christmas night. I've never gone, not even once!"

Olivia Crimmins sighed. In truth, she hated these vacations as much as Neddie did. Islands bored her. She spent most of the time feeling guilty about how much money they had compared to the people who lived there. And since birth all Neddie had known of Christmas was a series of expensive resorts in hot climates, with nobody his age to play with. Every year, Olivia Crimmins was torn between a husband who hated to be in Ryland Falls on Christmas Day and a son who hated to leave.

She looked across the breakfast table at her husband, who was still waiting for her to answer.

"Well," she said dispiritedly, "I was thinking that we haven't been to St. Maarten's in a while. Perhaps we could get one of those guesthouses on the beach."

"Hmmf," said Edward Crimmins, whose mind was already thinking ahead to the morning conference with his sales manager. "Sounds good to me. Why don't you go ahead and make a reservation." He took a piece of toast from the toast rack and buttered it absentmindedly. Something was on his calendar for this evening, but he couldn't remember what it was.

"Are we doing anything tonight?"

"We definitely are," said Olivia Crimmins. "At six o'clock. Open House at Neddie's school."

"Oh, right!" Edward Crimmins exclaimed. Reaching across the table, he snatched the cereal box away from Neddie's face and smiled at him. "Are we going to see a lot of gold stars and blue ribbons tonight, Neddie boy?"

Neddie's heart jumped at the words *blue ribbons* and then relaxed. Mr. Campbell had sworn he wouldn't tell anybody, not even the principal. But before Neddie could answer, Edward Crimmins glanced at his watch and saw that he was late. Flinging down his napkin, he pushed himself away from the table and stood up.

"Time to go," he announced, scooping up his watch and dropping it back into his vest pocket. He kissed his wife and brushed the top of Neddie's head with his hand as he passed his chair.

"Six o'clock," he said to no one in particular. "Six o'clock . . . I'll be there."

But he wasn't.

Not at six o'clock, when all the other parents were pouring into the school and Neddie took up his position in front of his drawing.

Not at six-thirty, when Neddie was still standing

there, straining his eyes down the hall for the first glimpse of his father.

And not at seven, when Olivia Crimmins called his office and demanded that the secretary interrupt his meeting.

"Your son," she whispered fiercely through her tears from a phone booth down the hall from the principal's office, "is standing beside his drawing—which won the school's first prize, Edward!—and he—is— *waiting* for you!"

She could not contain her sobbing. Holding the phone with one shoulder against her ear, she leaned against the side of the booth and let the tears spill through her fingers as Edward Crimmins battled to control them at the other end. But his words had no connective thread: "important"—"couldn't cancel"— "tell Neddie"—"can't afford."

She interrupted, "His heart is broken, Edward." She leaned her head against the wall and whispered into the phone, "I'm not sure I can bear it, Edward. I'm not sure I can."

Hanging up the phone, Olivia Crimmins wiped

her eyes, then strode down the hall to where Neddie was standing.

"Neddie," she said, trying to make her voice even, "I want you to know that I am so proud of you. And that even if your drawing hadn't won first prize—which it definitely deserved—I think it is the most original and wonderful picture you have ever made."

"Why didn't Dad come?" Neddie asked.

Kneeling down, she put her arms around him and looked him in the eye. "Your father said . . . your father said that he . . ." It was no use. She could not get the words to line up in her mouth the right way. She began to cry.

Neddie had never seen his mother cry and it frightened and embarrassed him. What if somebody saw them? "That's okay, Mom," he whispered, "that's okay." He pushed against her arms, but she only hugged him tighter. "Mom! Please! I want to go home."

*

That night, it got so cold in Ryland Falls that the seams in the sidewalk outside of All Saints Church buckled. A branch from an elm tree behind the feed store abruptly broke off and pierced the tin roof like a dagger. The pipes burst beneath Elwood's Market. And a crack where none had been before appeared on Neddie Crimmins's heart.

A crack in the heart of an eight-year-old boy is not a very noticeable thing on earth. For one thing, there are so many eight-year-olds. For another, most of them have a rather small vocabulary. They don't have the words to call attention to their condition. But in that other place where all cracked, broken, lost, and hardened hearts are recorded, it was noticed right away. And when Neddie Crimmins's heart was placed gently upon the scale with all the other damaged hearts in Ryland Falls, it was considered one heart too many.

That night the snow that was scheduled to fall didn't. The next day, the sky was the color of pavement, dull and lifeless, like the color of Neddie's eyes.

# Chapter Six

MIRANDA BRIDGEMAN opened up her nightstand drawer and took out her diary. Skipping over the empty pages to "December 7," she uncapped her pen, tapped it thoughtfully against her recently straightened front teeth, and began to write.

"My Christmas List." That was as far as she got.

"Miranda," called her mother from downstairs. "Come bring your grandmother her breakfast tray."

"I'm busy," yelled Miranda from behind her bedroom door.

"And I'm waiting," said her mother, who was expecting another baby and expected Miranda to help.

She stuffed her diary back in the drawer and stomped down the stairs. Do this, do that! Ever since her grandmother had moved in, she had twice as much work to do. She wished her grandmother lived on another planet.

Miranda Bridgeman was eleven years old and full of wishes—to have long, straight hair instead of short, curly hair, to be a championship figure skater, to live someplace other than Ryland Falls where she would have a chance to start over with a new, improved personality. Miranda's life was layered with wishes, the way her bedroom floor was layered with clothes, and somewhere beneath the tangle was the small brass key that came with the diary.

"If you'd hang your clothes up," sighed Miranda's

mother, "you'd probably find all kinds of things you're looking for."

But the one thing Miranda knew she would not find on the bedroom floor was the thing she wanted most—an interesting life. Where things happened! Things that she could write about. The diary had been a big disappointment in this regard.

Miranda had thought that if she had a special place to record interesting experiences, then the odds of having interesting experiences would increase. But that's not the way it had turned out. "Cleaned the parakeet cage," read one entry. "Got my braces off at the dentist" was another. "My grandmother broke her hip and is moving in with us."

Miranda's life was not diary material, so she rarely recorded it. It didn't matter that the key was lost. Miranda had nothing to hide except her fear of the dark, and that wasn't something she would ever write about. At eleven years old, she knew she was supposed to be over it. Fact: witches do not hide under the bed waiting to snatch your ankles. Fact: there are no robbers hiding in the closet. Still, she needed a night-light to fall asleep. That was another fact.

Miranda carried the tray into her grandmother's room. Morning sun streaked through the blinds, across the faded photographs on the wall and the corner cabinet full of antique Chinese fans above a wing chair by the window. Everything in the room was old, including Pasha, a great big puffball of a Persian cat her grandmother doted upon. In human years, Pasha was about the same age as Miranda, but her grandmother liked Pasha better. Miranda set the tray down, none too quietly, and left the room.

Miranda's grandmother kept her eyes closed so she wouldn't have to talk to her granddaughter. She didn't know what to say. For three months she had been trying to figure out what to say, but Miranda was a tough case to crack, not that she had much opportunity to study her. Most of the time Miranda was just a blur running past her bedroom door, on her way to school or a friend's house. And when she was home, she was usually in her room, talking on the phone, or sulking.

When Miranda sulked, it was an awful thing. Gloom poured out of her eyes, gathered in a puddle around her feet, left tracks around the house, and seeped out from beneath her bedroom door when she was on the silent, sulking side of it.

Mrs. Bridgeman slid her foot back and forth beneath the covers until she found Pasha, curled up in a warm lump at the bottom of the bed. She sat up and poured herself a cup of tea. Outside, the school bus braked to a stop in front of the house. Pulling aside the curtain, she watched Miranda trudge down the walk and climb on board.

Miranda was a pretty little girl, but in Mrs. Bridgeman's opinion, spoiled. Her dolls slept in better beds than most real babies. Her mother never made her clean up her room, which looked like a Turkish rag market. Not that she'd ever been to a Turkish rag market, but she could imagine it.

Pasha picked his way delicately up the blanket and settled in at her side. Poor Pasha. It had been a shock for him to come into a strange house where the dog spent most of the time trying to chase him outside.

"Sweet thing," she murmured, idly stroking his fur. The tea was making her feel less cranky.

Maybe I shouldn't be so hard on Miranda, her grandmother thought. After all, she was only eleven years old, and looking back, which is what she spent most of the time doing these days, Mrs. Bridgeman remembered that she hadn't been such a sweet little girl when she was Miranda's age either. In fact, she was quite a handful, always tugging at the leash wanting to get out from under the rest of the family so she could explore the world without a chaperon. Perhaps Miranda and she were cut from the same cloth.

On the wall above Mrs. Bridgeman's bed was a photograph of her own grandmother whom she had adored. She had spent every free minute sitting in her grandmother's room, asking for stories. But maybe that was because there wasn't any television. Maybe girls Miranda's age have so many more ways to entertain themselves these days that grandmothers are deadwood. She had to admit she felt like deadwood much of the time.

She reached for the newspaper on the tray. It was

full of Christmas ads. Perhaps she should think about what to get Miranda, not that she approved of the way parents loaded it up around the tree every year for children.

As she leafed through the paper, idly wishing her hot-water bottle wasn't cold, her eye was caught by a sale on electric heating pads. She would ask her daughter-in-law to pick up one for her this afternoon. The morning sun was beginning to warm up the room, and Mrs. Bridgeman felt tired again. Letting the newspaper slip to the floor, she drew Pasha up like a muff against her cheek and went back to sleep. She would think about Christmas tomorrow.

# Chapter Seven

FRANCES NICKERSON had the sharpest eyes in town. Seeing beneath the surface was a skill she had developed when she had taught school and had to read children's faces daily. Now that she was retired, she didn't have the same need. But the habit of noticing things had stuck with her.

On the morning of December 14, she was in

Elwood's Market waiting for her groceries to be rung up. "Haven't you been gaining a little weight lately?" she asked Diane, behind the counter.

Diane frowned. "I'm always gaining a little weight, except when I'm losing a little weight."

Frances Nickerson smiled sympathetically. "Yes, well, I guess you're in a gaining phase."

Later she saw Tommy Elwood park in the three-minute zone in front of the post office.

"You're going to get a ticket," she warned.

"I'll only be a minute," said Tommy, who had some Christmas hams to mail.

"It only takes a minute to get a ticket," she replied. And sure enough, there it was, fluttering like a pink paper tongue beneath the windshield wiper, when he returned.

If there was something to notice, Frances Nickerson noticed it first and told you about it, even if you didn't want to know. And for the past two weeks, her powers of observation had been on high alert. Something was wrong in Ryland Falls this Christmas, and she couldn't finger the cause.

The Christmas decorations in the stores were distinctly uninspired—a few colored lights, a little spray-on snow, but nothing extra. The library didn't have its usual display of popular Christmas stories in the front window. And the columns on the front porch of the inn, always wrapped with festive swags of fir and gold ribbon for the holidays, were inexplicably bare.

On her daily walks around town, Frances couldn't help but notice that the residents weren't holding up their end of Christmas either: not as many candles in front windows, fewer reindeer on the lawns. And from what little she could see through the Crimminses' bay window, their Christmas tree wasn't even up yet. And where was the other smaller tree they always set out on the second-floor balcony?

"Have you noticed," she asked the postman, when he handed her the mail, "that there aren't as many Christmas cards in the delivery this year?"

"Come to think of it," he said, "you're right. So far, I've only gotten one from my insurance agent and my brother-in-law in Montana."

"Hmm," she said, gazing across the street. The

Bridgemans' front door didn't have a wreath on it. Then again, neither did her own.

The holiday season in Ryland Falls was not progressing in its usual enthusiastic way. People dutifully untangled the Christmas lights, got out the ornaments, made the usual lists of which child wanted what toy, and so on. But the preparations felt tedious, like reading a boring book for a book report, or cleaning out the hall closet.

Perhaps, thought Frances Nickerson, it's the lack of snow. As far back as anybody could remember, there had always been a decent covering on the ground by December. But it was the middle of the month now, and every morning the children woke up and looked out the window, hoping snow had finally come during the night. They pressed their noses against the panes and dreamed of snowy things—snowball fights, and snowmen, and slapping their sleds down upon snow-covered hills and racing to the bottom. But all they saw were the same old leftover autumn leaves and empty acorn shells skittering with the wind across the ground. One gray and snowless day followed the next, and even the grown-ups trudged behind, as if they were in the grip of a low-grade spell that made them do things they didn't want to, and not do things they did.

"What's the matter with me?" sighed one woman as she sank into a tub full of gardenia-scented bubble bath she thought she had bought for her daughter's Christmas stocking.

"I shouldn't do this," said a man as he strapped a new alligator watchband around his wrist. When he had taken early leave from work, he had thought he was going downtown to buy presents for his wife and mother-in-law.

The shops were full of people drifting around the aisles looking for gifts. But there was no real accounting for the fact that, day after day, they came home with presents they regretted buying, no presents at all, or—most shocking of all—presents for themselves.

Frances Nickerson always made a pyramid of red apples and boxwood for a holiday centerpiece. Picking through the apple bin at Elwood's for the best ones, she said to Diane, "I don't know, but I have the nagging feeling that Christmas isn't going to amount to much this year."

"It would be fine with me if it didn't amount to *anything*," grumped Diane. "With my daughter out of work and three grandchildren wanting every toy on the planet . . ."

Frances Nickerson wished she hadn't brought the subject up. "Well," she soothed, "I'm sure it's nice to have them all with you during the holidays."

"I guess . . . if my oil furnace hadn't just broke on me. I'm tired!"

Grumpy Diane was not an optimist and Frances Nickerson wasn't listening anyway. But when Diane declared that she was tired, she was speaking for the entire town.

There were very few holiday parties. With only two entries, the Parent-Teacher Association decided to cancel the gingerbread-house contest. And three of the five families who had said they would be part of the Christmas house tour canceled because they just didn't have the energy. Even the pleasant events, where all anyone had to do was sit back and be inspired, felt like work.

December 18 was the night of the annual *Messiah* sing-along at All Saints Church. But at the last minute, Miranda Bridgeman's parents decided to order take-out Chinese and make an early night of it instead. What the Bridgemans didn't know was that half the people who had planned to be there had decided, in the same last-minute way, to do the same thing.

Reverend Williams always looked forward to the *Messiah* night as the high point of his year as rector. But this Christmas, there weren't even enough people to sing the alto parts. Later, as he was locking the church doors, he said to his wife, "Well, I must say, I've certainly seen better attendance."

"Maybe there's a flu bug going around," she offered.

"The Bridgemans always come. I wonder if they were sick."

"Not too sick to be ordering take-out Chinese," said Mrs. Williams, who had been picking up the choir robes at the cleaner's next door and seen Mr. Bridgeman getting into his car with some cartons of chow mein and egg rolls.

Reverend Williams was beginning to feel professionally threatened and decided to change the subject. "Maybe it's time to get the tree tomorrow."

"You mean," said Mrs. Williams quietly, "maybe it's time for *you* to get the tree tomorrow."

For twenty-three years, Mrs. Williams had been told by her husband she could get the tree without him, and suddenly she didn't see it as such a privilege anymore.

Who was going to get the tree was a question that seemed to preoccupy everyone. Remarks like "If it depends on me to get it, I will decorate a coatrack!" or "I'm tired of being blamed for every bare spot" flew around town. Meanwhile, December 25 was getting closer, and an unexpected surplus of Christmas trees was on Giovanni's lot.

On the night of December 21, Giovanni sat by his woodstove counting up the day's disappointing receipts. Only three trees had been sold since early morning when he'd started waiting with growing anxiety for a last-minute influx of customers who never came.

After feeding Max and adjusting the dampers on

his woodstove, he closed the flaps of his tent, slipped beneath the pile of blankets on his cot, and turned on his portable radio.

"Snow is forecast," said the weatherman, though he didn't sound as if he believed his own forecast. Giovanni raised himself on one elbow to check the level of wood in his stove. It was full. Turning off his radio, he lay in the dark and wondered whether next year he should take his trees to a better town.

In his apartment above Elwood's Market, Will Campbell lay in bed wondering where he was going to find a new job.

Across town, Miranda Bridgeman gazed out her window at the streetlights below and wondered whether it was more poetic to call them a "string of pearls" or a "chain of diamonds."

And on the third floor of the Crimmins house, Neddie Crimmins wondered why he felt as if something big was about to happen.

By midnight, every wondering man, woman, and child in Ryland Falls was fast asleep.

Then the snow began to fall.

# *Chapter Eight*

IT FELL SOFTLY, like talcum powder from a shaker. Slowly, carefully, it dusted every roof and road, sifting back and forth with the wind until every inch of Ryland Falls was as white as a baker's apron. Then, once the town was covered, the snow began to fill it up.

Window boxes, birdbaths, the spaces between fence

pickets, flake by flake, the snow piled higher, sweeping against tree trunks, climbing up the branches. Front and back steps disappeared. Garbage cans turned into mushrooms. Cars, hedges, and fire hydrants were buried.

All night long, the snow fell silently from the sky, until Ryland Falls groaned beneath the weight of it. And on the morning of December 22, when the sun pulled itself up over the top of Old Rag Mountain and tried, in vain, to shine upon the town, it was still coming down.

Will Campbell woke up colder than he had ever before been in his entire life. He sat up and looked outside. The window ledge was piled high with snow, the panes crazed with frost. The heat pump must have gone off during the night. He pulled on his clothes, wrapped a muffler around his neck, and clambered down the stairs.

The first floor of the market was just as cold. He unlocked the front door and pushed it open against the snowdrifts piled against it. A thin wisp of smoke curled from the stovepipe jutting through the roof of Giovanni's tent. Will trudged toward it.

Inside, Giovanni sat with Max by his woodstove listening to his portable radio. "Well, folks," said the reporter, "this is a big one! And it took us so-called weather experts completely by surprise. Three feet of snow so far and no end in sight."

Giovanni heard somebody calling from outside. Opening the tent flap, he saw the tall young man who lived above the market.

"My heat's out," said Will. "Any chance I could warm up by your stove while I figure out what to do next?"

Giovanni nodded and motioned him inside. The tent was as warm as toast, and Will's eye took appreciative note of the neat and orderly way the woodsman had arranged everything in it.

"I don't have much of a seat to offer," said Giovanni, rolling the stump end of a log next to the stove and putting a pillow on it, "but you're welcome to it—and some coffee, too."

"Any port in a storm," said Will, "and I'm grateful for it." Giovanni handed him a steaming mug.

"All government offices are closed," the radio

reported. "Stores will open two hours late . . . at least! And schools are canceled."

December 22 would have been the last day of school before Christmas vacation. Now, Will would not have to tell the children he wasn't returning. As he sipped his coffee, he looked over the rim of the mug and saw an old brown book lying by Giovanni's cot. He could just make out the title on the spine: *World Famous Paintings.* He knew the book well!

"So," he said, "are you an artist, too?"

Giovanni shook his head. "No, no, I just like to look at the pictures."

Will nodded. "So did I. That book was what made me want to be a painter before I even knew how to read. But I lost it a long time ago. Where'd you get yours?"

"It belonged to my wife."

"Mind if I have a look? I never thought I'd see another copy."

Giovanni nodded and handed him the book. Giovanni had stared at every painting in it so many times that he had made up stories about each one. It fell open on Will's lap to *The Virgin and Child and Donor* by Jan van Eyck.

"I remember this one," said Will.

Giovanni pulled his chair closer and looked down at the page. "That's the picture I look at most. I've never seen anything like it. But it don't look like Jesus and Mary to me. Not the way they're dressed up like that."

"Well, the woman was probably one of the artist's girlfriends or favorite models. And the man sitting across from them in the funny bowl haircut? He's the man who paid to have himself painted into the picture."

"So he isn't part of the story?"

"No," said Will, "he just wanted the people who saw the picture to think he was a holy man. But he wasn't. He was just a rich man."

"He has a mean face. That's what I always think when I look at him."

They fell silent, looking at the painting together.

"Is that angel in the corner somebody who paid to be in the picture, too?" Giovanni asked.

Will chuckled. "I don't know. But whenever there's a Nativity scene, the painter will usually stick an angel in somewhere."

Will realized that he hadn't introduced himself. He held out his hand. "My name's Will Campbell and I'm a painter, but not in this league. I'm a failed painter, at least so far."

Giovanni took Will's hand shyly and then dropped it. Rarely had he done so much talking to another human being in one stretch.

"I'm Giovanni," he said, not adding what he thought—that with a lot full of unsold trees, he was a failure, too.

"I'm glad to meet you," said Will. And he was.

Giovanni was the first adult Will had met since moving to Ryland Falls who loved art as much as he did. Then again, Giovanni didn't live in Ryland Falls, and after Christmas, neither would Will.

# *Chapter Nine*

By NOON ON THE twenty-second, the snow had reached four feet. Miranda Bridgeman was thrilled. At last she had something exciting to write about in her diary.

"This is not a snowstorm! This is a snow catastrophe! As if archangels had grabbed the four corners of the sky like a bedsheet and dumped all the snow meant for everywhere in the world right on us!"

Miranda studied the words she'd just written. That's exactly how it felt and she liked the way she had expressed it. She put her diary away and walked down the hall. Her grandmother was watching television in her room. Miranda stood in the doorway and watched, too.

"The trucks are out now trying to clear the roads," said a reporter who was barely visible in a blur of flakes, "but it's coming down faster than they can plow. And the supply of rock salt—" Just then the screen went blank.

"Oh, my goodness," said Miranda's grandmother, "do you think we've blown a fuse?"

"No," called Miranda's mother from downstairs. "The town just lost its power. I'm going to try to dig the car out and go downtown for some supplies."

By noon all the stores were sold out of batteries, candles, kerosene, and cans of Sterno. Summer lanterns were taken out of storage. People were hauling in firewood to use in their fireplaces to heat food and water if they didn't have a gas stove.

"This is getting serious," wrote Miranda, who made a grilled-cheese sandwich for lunch by holding a frying pan over the fire in the fireplace. "It's like we're back in the 18th century or something."

That night, the people of Ryland Falls ate by candlelight and went to bed carrying candles or flashlights. As Miranda lay in bed, listening to the scrape of snowplows moving up and down the street, she tried hard not to think about the darkness. But the harder she tried, the darker the room got, until the excitement of the day gave way to the fear of the night and Miranda's heart started to beat in her chest like a drum. It was not only dark in her room, but in the whole house, and the whole town beyond that. Certainly a robber would have a field day.

Miranda's grandmother heard the door creak. Then she saw a small person standing by her bed.

"Miranda?"

The small person nodded.

"Do you need something? What's the matter?"

"I was wondering," whispered Miranda, "if I could . . ."

Mrs. Bridgeman didn't wait for her to finish. "Get warm under this quilt? It must be freezing. You don't have enough blankets." She moved over in the bed, let Miranda slip in beside her, and together they stared at the ceiling as if it were the most interesting object in the world.

"Grandma," said Miranda, breaking the silence, "have you ever been in a storm this serious before?"

"No, but I was in a flood that was pretty bad."

"Where?" Miranda couldn't imagine her grandmother being anywhere but in her room, sitting beneath her Chinese fan collection.

"In Kentucky. I was trying to lead a sick horse through the mountains and we got caught in a rainstorm."

Miranda's imagination could barely take in all this new information about her grandmother. Leading a horse through the mountains? What mountains?

"I was a frontier nurse who took care of people who couldn't afford a doctor. But I wound up taking care of anything that was willing to trust its luck with me—horses, pigs, cows, cats. One time I carried a newborn baby boy in a saddlebag all the way to the hospital."

"Were you ever scared?"

"Sometimes. Yes, I have to say, sometimes I was. But I was more afraid of having a dull life. I wanted to do something different, something that wasn't what everybody else did."

"I think about that, too," said Miranda.

"I know. I recognize that in you."

"I want to be a writer." Miranda had never told anybody this before.

"A writer!" exclaimed her grandmother. "Well, now, that ought to provide you with an interesting life—what do you want to write about?"

"I don't know. I just like to describe things."

"Then you've got the right impulse for the profession. Describing things is what a writer has to do."

Pasha came purring up the length of the bed and settled himself in a crease between Miranda and her grandmother.

"I think Pasha's feeling a little left out," said Mrs. Bridgeman, giving Pasha a pat.

Miranda wanted to hear more about the sick horse and the rainstorm, but was feeling too warm and drowsy to listen. "Will you tell me more stories about your life tomorrow?"

"If you're still interested."

But Miranda didn't answer. She was already fast asleep, her nose buried in Pasha's fur.

# Chapter Ten

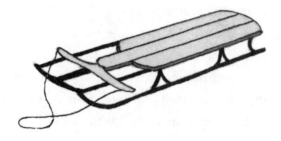

ON THE MORNING of December 23, Edward Crimmins paced around and around the living room like a caged bear. Outside, his car was buried beneath a hard crust of snow. Twice, he had tried to clear a path to it from the front steps, only to see the car disappear beneath new snow almost as soon as he put away the shovel. Now, the phones didn't work. He couldn't get in touch with anybody outside the house. He couldn't get in touch with anybody *inside* the house, either.

"Olivia!" There was no answer.

"Neddie!" More silence.

"Where is everybody!" he muttered.

He walked into the kitchen. It was still snowing, and without the overhead light on, the kitchen had a gray, ghostly look. This was the second day Ryland Falls had been without electricity. Breakfast had been cold cereal and instant coffee heated up on a Sterno can. Lunch was canned chili and fruit cocktail. He took the last banana from the fruit bowl and frowned at it.

The airport was closed and his plane had been hauled into a hangar for safekeeping. This banana would be as close as he would get to a tropical vacation this Christmas. He took a bite and gazed out the kitchen window.

At the far end of the garden he could see Neddie loading logs from the woodpile onto his sled. The only reliable source of heat downstairs was the fireplace in the living room. Yesterday, Olivia had hung blankets across both entrances to trap the warmth.

Edward Crimmins took out his pocket watch and looked at it. It was noon, but the snow had made time irrelevant. Nobody could go anywhere or do anything, so there was really no need to know what time it was. Two days before Christmas, Ryland Falls had come to a complete halt. Edward Benchley Crimmins had come to a complete halt, too.

Well, he thought, putting his watch away, there was nothing left to do but wait it out. As he stood in the kitchen and watched Neddie struggle to pull a heavy sledful of logs toward the house, he felt a strange, totally unexplained urge to cry. Dimly, he remembered another sled from a long time ago, when he had felt this same sense of helplessness.

Edward Crimmins didn't know this, but he was one of many people in Ryland Falls who found themselves thinking about things that made them weepy. The silence encouraged it. Sealed within their houses and away from the outer lives and responsibilities that defined and distracted them, they were forced toward a solitude and separateness that most of them had never had to confront for long. Silence was a spade that dug down in the soft soil of people's memories and brought things up—faces, conversations, relationships, feelings that had been buried, like stones in a farmer's field.

A grown man wanting to cry? What on earth is the matter with me? thought Edward Crimmins. I haven't wanted to cry in years. And I don't want to cry now! What he did want, suddenly, was to be with Neddie. He grabbed his parka off the peg.

Outside, Neddie stood with his sled and looked up at the sky, swirling with flakes. He imagined it as a giant piece of paper being cut into countless tiny bits. When all the bits had drifted to the ground, the sky would start over, with a new sheet, the way artists start over with fresh paper in a sketchpad. Then he saw his father coming toward him, and the next thing he felt was a giant, wool-covered glove wrapped around his own on the rope handle of the sled.

"Two pulling this thing will make it easier," said his father.

Together they dragged the logs to the back porch,

brushed the snow off them, and carried them inside. Then, when the work was done, Edward Crimmins took Neddie Crimmins sledding.

A large man taking a small boy sledding in a snowstorm is not a particularly remarkable sight. That day, Cemetery Hill was full of sleds, some of them carrying fathers who sat with their sons just the way Edward Crimmins sat with Neddie, the father's boots braced against the handlebars and Neddie sitting between his knees, as if they were the arms of a chair.

But in that other place, where the smallest act of generosity is noted, and the quietest act of courage is heard, events were set in motion that had been waiting a long time for Edward Crimmins to read his lines correctly.

That night, the Crimmins family ate in front of the living room fireplace. The main dish was hot dogs skewered on the ends of wire hangers held over the flames.

"I must say, Olivia," said her husband, "you have made a room without any heat or electricity very comfortable."

With candles burning on the mantel, a fire in the

grate, and soft yellow light flickering against the walls and curtains, the room was as cozy and richly colored as an oil painting. Mrs. Crimmins sat with her knitting in a wing chair by the fire. Mr. Crimmins sat in front of it, with Neddie, as he had been on the sled, between his knees.

Edward Crimmins had not felt this peaceful in a long time. Yet the same feeling of wanting to cry rose up in him again.

He wrapped his arms around Neddie a little tighter and cleared his throat. "Did I ever tell you the story about the sled my father gave me one Christmas?"

"When?" asked Neddie.

"I was about your age. Only we didn't have any money for things like sleds."

"How did your father find it, then?"

"He didn't. He made it himself. Every night for about three weeks before Christmas he would come home from work and disappear into his basement workroom, and none of us was allowed to go down there and see what he was doing. Then, on Christmas morning, there it was beneath the tree."

"Was it a good sled?"

Edward Crimmins began to chuckle at the memory. "Oh, yes, it was beautiful all right. It was the most beautiful sled I had ever seen. It had shiny brass runners, and bright red handlebars, and smooth, perfectly sanded wooden slats to lie upon. He even painted my name in black letters down the middle. But there was just one problem. . . ."

"What?"

"The sled didn't work."

"What do you mean it didn't work?"

"When we took the sled to Cemetery Hill, it wouldn't go down the hill."

"Why?"

"It was too heavy."

Edward Crimmins began to rock back and forth in front of the fire, as if he were cradling something terribly sad or wonderfully terrible in his lap. The memory of his crestfallen father, standing at the bottom of Cemetery Hill, watching his son try to make the sled go, filled him with a kind of desperate pity.

"What happened to the sled?" asked Neddie.

"I don't know. All I remember is that the sled didn't work and it was because my father was poor and I felt sorry for him and I didn't want to grow up and be poor, too."

"Edward," said Olivia Crimmins quietly from the sofa, "you've never told me that story before."

"I had forgotten it."

All over Ryland Falls, people were remembering things they had forgotten, memories that had frozen the heart and made it hard to feel or remember anything. But sitting in a dark room before a warm fire with his father's arms around him, Neddie's heart burned with happiness. He leaned back against his father's chest, and in one of those silent exchanges of heat that can't be seen, Edward Crimmins's own heart began to melt.

# *Chapter Eleven*

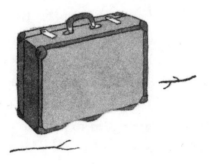

EARLY ON THE MORNING of December 24, seven-year-old Anna Aragon and her mother climbed aboard a large bus full of passengers. It was going to be a long trip with many stops, and theirs would be the last one. But Anna didn't care how long it took. The important part was that they were leaving. She leaned against her mother, who shook a thick shawl around Anna's shoulders, and went to sleep.

Anna Aragon was smart, strong, and tough. She had to be. Drug dealers hid their supplies in the bushes outside their row house. There were neighborhood gunfights and police chases. One night as she lay in bed, she heard a loud thump, as if somebody had fallen from a ladder or dropped a sack full of bricks on the front porch. She was too scared to look out the window, but the next morning, when she opened the front door, there was a man, lying in a pool of blood.

"He's dead," she signed to her deaf mother. That night, Anna's mother sat down at the kitchen table and wrote to Anna's grandmother, who lived in another city two hundred miles away. "We cannot live here anymore," she wrote. "Anna needs to grow up in a safer place. I will try to get a job that will help pay for our expenses if you will please let us come and stay."

Anna's grandmother had written back immediately. They were to come for Christmas. They could live with her.

As soon as they received the letter, Anna and her mother threw out what they didn't want, packed what they did, and took everything else of value to the local pawnshop. The money from the pawnbroker paid the last month's rent and bought two bus tickets. Before they left the house for their trip, Anna's mother counted out three bills and put them in Anna's jacket pocket. As Anna slept, she kept one hand curled around them, until the voice of the driver from the front of the bus woke her up.

"Miss . . . miss."

Anna sat up and looked around. Her mother was asleep. They were the only people left in the bus. It was nearly dark and snowing hard. Dimly, Anna could see a sign outside, "Elwood's Market." But no lights were on in the store.

"Where are we?" she asked the bus driver.

"Ryland Falls."

"When do we get off?"

"It's the stop after this one, but I'm not going over no mountain in this kind of mess." The driver shook a fist at the snow. "If I knew I had this waiting for me,

I wouldn't have started out this morning. I figure if we turn around right now, we can make it back to where we came from before the roads are totally covered over. But we can't get over Old Rag tonight. No way, José!"

Anna's mother was awake now and looking at the driver.

"Ma'am," the driver said, "you need to tell me what you want to do. You can get off here or come on back with the bus and start over tomorrow. It don't make no difference to me."

Anna had to think fast. "I'll talk to my mother," she said.

The bus driver shrugged, draped his arms over the steering wheel, and stared out the window. Quickly, Anna rearranged the bus driver's words and passed them on. She couldn't bear to turn back now.

"He says we have to get off here," she signed.

Her mother's eyes widened. "Here?" she signed. "Where are we?"

"Almost to Grandma's," signed Anna, "but the bus can't get over the mountain. So we have to stay here somewhere tonight and then get another bus tomorrow."

"Where?" her mother signed.

Anna looked her mother in the eye and put on her most sincere expression. "The bus driver said he would help us."

It wasn't really a lie. She was just telling her mother what the bus driver would say once she asked for his help.

Walking to the front of the bus, she planted herself in front of him and reported the conversation with her mother she hadn't actually had. "My mother says we'll stay here and that she'd like you to find us a place."

The driver shifted irritably in his seat. Who did they think he was!

"Well, now," he said sarcastically, "I don't guess I know where that place would be. This town looks shut down, and I'm not in the business of being no tour director."

"We're staying. That's what my mother said."

The driver threw up his hands. "I'll get your bag."

Anna stepped off the bus into a swirl of snow.

There were no lights anywhere, except for a fire in a wire trash can on a Christmas tree lot across the street. She was beginning to lose her courage. Against her will, she felt tears well up in her eyes. No way was she going to ruin everything by crying, but it was freezing cold and in a few minutes she and her mother would be standing in the snow, without anyplace to go.

"Okay," said the bus driver, dropping the suitcase with a thump at Anna's feet. "What's your plan?"

A sob came ripping out of her throat. "I don't know. Listen, we can't go back, because we don't have any place to go back to. We only got a place to *get to*."

Now tears were running down her cheeks. The bus driver was taken aback.

"Look, kid," he pleaded, "I didn't get you into this, and I don't see how I can get you out of it."

Just then, he saw a man emerge from the tent across the street and throw a bucket of ashes on the snow. Maybe he'd know of something that was open.

"Come on," the driver said to Anna, who was still crying, "I don't have all day." Then he called out to Giovanni, "Halloo."

Giovanni looked up and saw a man pulling a little girl and a big suitcase across the street toward him.

"Got a little problem here," said the bus driver, setting down the suitcase in front of the tent. "My bus won't make it across the mountain where this kid and her mother need to go. You know of where they might spend the night?"

Giovanni shook his head. "Nothing in Ryland Falls is open. We've been without electricity for three days, and everything's shut down. You'd best go back where you came from."

"My mother said we can't go back," said Anna quietly. "We got to keep on going."

The bus driver was getting desperate. If he didn't turn the bus around soon, he'd be stuck in Ryland Falls, too. Peering around the flap of the tent, he saw a cot, a lantern, and a woodstove inside.

"Look," he said to Giovanni, "I know this might be a little unusual, but you got a decent place here. I mean, it's rough, but you got what you need. Is there any chance they might be able to stay here—just for the night?"

Giovanni's eyes widened. The idea of having a little girl and her mother was unthinkable. "Oh, no, this is no place for them."

Anna dug into her jacket pocket and brought out her tiny roll of bills. "We can pay you," she said, holding out the money.

Giovanni shook his head. "Oh, no, I couldn't charge anybody."

The bus driver grabbed at the opening. "Does that mean you'll let them stay?"

Giovanni looked at Anna. He could tell, from the way she was holding her chin up, that she was trying to keep the tears in her eyes from spilling down her face. She had the same wobbly-legged look that Max had had when he'd found him at the dump.

"You'd be warm enough," he said, "but . . ."

Anna didn't wait to hear more. She turned around and raced back to the bus to get her mother.

"Thanks, mister," said the bus driver. "Merry Christmas."

Giovanni picked up the suitcase. Nothing about this Christmas had gone the way he'd wanted. "Well,

Max," he said, "we've got company," and he had no sooner set down the suitcase on top of the cot than they were standing in the doorway—a small, dark-eyed little girl holding on to her mother's hand as if her mother were the child.

"Come in," he said. But Anna and her mother didn't move.

Anna stared at Max. "Does he bite?"

Giovanni reached down and held Max by his collar. "You don't have to be scared of him. He's a gentle dog."

Slowly, not taking her eyes off Max, Anna edged her way around him into the tent and sat down with her mother on the cot. "I'm scared of dogs."

Giovanni smiled. "You won't be scared of Max for very long. "

Anna's mother reached in her purse and took out a pad of paper and a pencil. Hastily she scribbled something down, tore it off, and handed it to Giovanni.

"My mother's deaf," explained Anna. "That's how she talks to people."

Anna's mother was looking at him, smiling expectantly.

"Go ahead, read it," said Anna. "Then you can write something back."

Giovanni handed the paper back to Anna, without looking up. "I'm not too good at reading. Or writing."

Anna gazed at Giovanni as if he were an interesting, but not very difficult, puzzle. "That's all right, you got hands." She held up her own. "That's how I talk to her, with my hands. I could show you."

It was a fair exchange. While Giovanni fixed a supper of pancakes, fried apples, and coffee, he told Anna about Max and how he had found him at the dump when he was a puppy, and Anna lost some of her fear. Anna showed Giovanni how to make different words with his fingers, and Giovanni lost some of his shyness.

Later, Anna and her mother curled up like spoons on the cot, beneath a pile of blankets. Max took his place on the floor beside them. Staring at him for a few minutes, then gathering up her courage, Anna reached out from beneath the blankets and gingerly brushed the top of his head with her fingers.

"What kind of dog is Max?"

"Mostly retriever," said Giovanni.

"What's that mean?"

"It means he knows how to pick up things, like birds, very gently, so nothing breaks, and bring them to you in his mouth."

Max gave Anna's hand a lick.

"Looks like you've made a new friend," said Giovanni.

"Does he watch out for you when you sleep?" Anna had never spent the night in such a strange, unguarded place before.

"That he does. And he'll watch out for you, too."

Soon Anna and her mother fell asleep while Giovanni dozed upright in a chair by the woodstove. Outside, in the swirling snow, the walls of the tent glowed like a lantern in the darkness.

Sometime during the night, after everybody in Ryland Falls was fast asleep, the last flake of snow shook itself from the sky.

# Chapter Twelve

ON CHRISTMAS MORNING, Ryland Falls woke up beneath a canopy of bright blue sky. As blue as Mary's cloak, thought Reverend Williams who had canceled the "Living Nativity" scene and now was trying, without success, to find the collapsed plywood manger. But the snow had so completely erased all the familiar landmarks that it was hard to find anything.

Reverend Williams stabbed up and down in the snow with the handle of his shovel. Some Christmas! he thought. With no electricity to power the organ, and no radiators to warm the church, there would be no worship service. He hit something hard and he began to dig. It was the sign in front of the church, with the title of today's undelivered sermon, "Oh, come all ye faithful!" Not without central heating, thought Reverend Williams.

This was the first time in the history of Ryland Falls that Christmas had been celebrated, or rather, not celebrated, under such emergency conditions. The electricity was still off. The phones were still not working. And the plows were so overwhelmed that the only street that was clear from one end to the other was Center Street. All the other roads were more like tracks between high drifts. The first thing people did on Christmas morning was to grab their shovels and dig toward each other.

All day long, Ryland Falls was full of the stamping of boots on newly cleared porches, and the voices of neighbors calling back and forth between houses.

Being able to see clearly across the street, instead of squinting through snow, was like suddenly sighting land after being marooned on the high seas.

Frances Nickerson hadn't been so excited since her school retirement party. As soon as she could make a path to the sidewalk, not that you could see the sidewalk, she set up a card table, spread it with a flowered cloth, and brought out some cups and cookies and hot tea in a thermos for whoever might like to join her.

"A tea party in the snow!" exclaimed Miranda's mother, who had always thought Frances Nickerson was a little odd. But now she knew it.

"I think it's very original," said Miranda.

"Why don't you shovel your way across the street and have a cup," said Miranda's grandmother. "I think we should show our support for the idea."

Other people, too, began to stumble out of their houses and toward their neighbors as if they had never seen each other so clearly—or dearly—before. How relaxed and unburdened everybody seemed, how straight their shoulders and open their expressions.

Neighbors who had not found the time to stop and

really talk to each other for many years suddenly had all the time in the world. And now it was not just Frances Nickerson who noticed things but many grown-ups, and children, too, who did. Being cooped up seemed to have sharpened everybody's eyes.

They noticed the way ice-coated tree branches clicked together like castanets, how the snow was milk blue in the shadows, and the way icicles hanging from the rain gutters trapped the light inside. Everything, from the soft scraping sound of a shovel to the shadow print of a tree against a garage door, seemed quietly remarkable. And they noticed something else, as well. The urge to chatter away about nothing seemed to have gone away. Everybody in Ryland Falls was quieter, as if the snow had pulled all the noise out of the air and buried it. And when they did speak, their words seemed to come from a deeper place inside.

But what nobody noticed until after Miranda's grandmother had woken from her afternoon nap was that Pasha was gone.

He wasn't curled up in his usual position at the end of the bed. He wasn't downstairs in the breakfast nook or on the living room sofa. All his favorite places were empty.

"Pasha? Pasha?" Every time Miranda's grandmother called his name, her voice trembled a little more. "I don't understand it. Pasha hates the snow. He'd never leave on his own."

Then she remembered what had woken her from her nap—the sound of the Bridgeman dog barking. The front door must have been open. He had chased Pasha outside.

"I'll go outside and look for her, Grandma," said Miranda. "I have sharp eyes."

All afternoon, Miranda trudged around the neighborhood—up and down the streets, into backyards, checking woodpiles, looking up into trees. But no cherished red blob of fur was to be seen anywhere. Just as the sun sank, Miranda came home.

Her grandmother was waiting at the front door. When she didn't see Pasha in Miranda's arms, she sank down in a chair and dropped her head into her hands.

"I'm sorry, Grandma," said Miranda.

"It's not your fault. Pasha had been cooped up for

too long. But if he doesn't come home tonight . . ." She couldn't finish the sentence.

That evening, the Bridgemans sat glumly around the kitchen table eating dinner—chicken noodle soup from a packet, canned okra, and green Jell-O with marshmallows that were as hard as bullets. Nobody complained. Only Pasha was on their minds.

Miranda looked out the window. Without any streetlights, she could barely see the road. But with a flashlight, she could make an arc of light upon the snow.

"Grandma," she said, "I can go out and look for Pasha some more with a flashlight."

"No!" said her mother firmly. "You will stay inside!"

"Not tonight," added her father. "It'll be well below freezing."

"I can't worry about you and Pasha, both," said her grandmother.

The idea of Pasha turning into an ice cube in the dark was horrible. But Miranda didn't want to turn into an ice cube in the dark either. When no one would allow her to go out again, Miranda was secretly relieved.

That night, she took the flashlight upstairs, got in bed, and made a warm tent of the covers where she could write in her diary. She had just uncapped her pen and written, "Christmas Night—very cold," when she heard a noise.

It was a soft, muffled sound she couldn't quite identify. Getting out of her bed, she tiptoed down the hall and followed the sound to her grandmother's bedroom door. Shivering in her bare feet, she listened intently. Her grandmother was crying into her pillow so no one would hear her. It was the saddest sound Miranda had ever heard.

Miranda tiptoed back into her room and stood there thinking. Then, she put on two pairs of wool socks and a suit of long underwear. On top of that she pulled on three sweaters and a pair of snow pants. Padding downstairs, she zipped herself into a parka, pulled on her boots and gloves, and quietly opened the back door.

Pulling the door shut quietly so nobody would

wake up, she heard the lock click and realized two terrible things at the same time. She had left the flashlight in her bedroom and she had locked herself out.

Standing between a locked door and the darkness, Miranda was terrified at what she'd done. But she couldn't bear the sound of her grandmother crying. She headed into the dark.

# Chapter Thirteen

WILL CAMPBELL turned up the wick on his lantern and held it above his head. By tomorrow morning, everything in his apartment had to be in a box or a suitcase. He looked around the room. It was a wreck of good intentions gone wrong—all the sketches that were meant to become paintings, all the paintings he didn't complete. On his desk was a stack of Christmas cards from his students. He couldn't bring himself to open them until he was in a new place and the pain of leaving Ryland Falls had lessened. He set the lantern down and went to work.

Outside, Giovanni was dragging all his unsold Christmas trees into the middle of the lot to make a bonfire. He was leaving tomorrow as soon as the road across Old Rag Mountain was cleared. Each tree he tossed upon the pile increased his regret. He had sold less than half his inventory, and the snow had left the remaining trees so wet that he would have to use his remaining kerosene to make them burn.

Ducking his head inside the tent, he said to Anna, "I'm going to make a bonfire. You and your mother can watch." Tying back the tent flaps, he moved the big wooden chair across the entrance so Anna could sit on her mother's lap and both could see. Then he wrapped mother and daughter in a heavy blanket against the cold.

Giovanni circled the pile of trees, carefully pouring kerosene around its base. Then he made another circle, pouring kerosene higher up in the wet branches to make sure the fire would catch. A bonfire of old Christmas trees wasn't much of an entertainment, but he might as well make it the best bonfire Anna had ever seen. He emptied the can.

Just then, Max appeared at Giovanni's side with an animal of some kind clasped between his jaws. Ever since the snow had stopped, Max had been busy scouting the neighborhood, expressing his retriever instinct.

"What have you got there?" Giovanni asked.

Max proudly laid his find at Giovanni's feet. Kneeling down to examine it, Giovanni wasn't sure it was alive or dead, but when he picked the small, limp creature off the ground and cradled it in his hand, the bedraggled little thing opened its eyes and mewed.

"Well," said Giovanni, carrying the cat over to show Anna and her mother, "Max has found a real prize."

"What is it?" asked Anna excitedly.

"A half-frozen, very wet little cat."

Anna held out her arms. "Let me have it," she begged. Gently, Giovanni deposited it in her lap.

Unbuttoning her jacket, Anna took Pasha, for that of course was his name, and rebuttoned it around him, leaving him just enough room to poke his head out from beneath Anna's chin.

"He's purring!" she announced solemnly.

"Just keep him right where he is," said Giovanni. "Between you and the bonfire, he should warm up soon." Taking out some matches, he bent down and lit the trees.

Slowly, surely, the fire caught hold, turning the pile of trees into a golden cone of light in the darkness. Giovanni stepped back behind Anna and her mother to watch as the bonfire popped and crackled and released the sweet smell of pitch into the air. Anna and her mother stared at it, transfixed.

Will Campbell saw light flickering on the walls of his apartment. Perhaps, he thought, the electricity has been restored. He stopped his packing and went to the window to see what the source of the light was. And there, right in front of him, was more illumination than he had seen in a long time.

The bonfire cast a wide circle of golden light upon

the snow, carved deep pockets of light and shadow on the blanket around the woman's shoulders, lit up the cheeks of the little girl on her lap. Soft light was coming from behind and around Giovanni as he stood in the entrance of the tent. And pushing in and out of the light was the darkness.

Will raised the window to see some more. Buttoned up in the little girl's jacket was a cat. Giovanni's dog was by her side, looking up at her. The mother was resting her chin on top of the little girl's head and gazing dreamily into the fire. Without taking his eyes off the scene, Will groped around his desk for a sketchpad and a charcoal pencil. Pulling up a chair to the open window, he rested his pad upon the sill and began to draw as quickly as he could.

\*

When Miranda Bridgeman first saw the light in the sky, she was trudging along, terrified. She didn't know what the light was, only that it looked warm and she thought that perhaps Pasha would have seen it, too. She ran toward it, slipping and sliding in the dark, teeth chattering and heart pounding. "Please, God," she prayed, "don't let me or Pasha freeze to death."

Neddie Crimmins and his father were just pulling on their boots and parkas. The town's sledding party on Cemetery Hill had been canceled along with everything else, but Neddie and his father were going anyway.

"Well, Neddie boy, your old man thought he was going to be eating mangoes on a beach tonight. It goes to show you shouldn't plan too far ahead."

"I thought I would be watching television in the hotel with a bad baby-sitter," said Neddie.

Edward Crimmins laughed and pushed his glasses up the bridge of his nose. "Not anymore. Let's go. We've got years of back sledding to catch up on."

As they reached the top of Cemetery Hill, Neddie saw a bright glow coming from Center Street. "Look, Dad. What's that?"

Edward Crimmins stared at it and shook his head. "I don't know, but it bears investigation. I hope nothing important is on fire. Let's take the sled downtown and see."

So it was that Miranda Bridgeman and Neddie and

Edward Crimmins headed for Giovanni's bonfire. But when they arrived, they discovered that quite a few other people in Ryland Falls had seen the light, as well.

Reverend Williams had just been getting undressed when he'd seen the glow out his bedroom window and decided to get dressed again and walk toward it. Mrs. Williams joined him.

Tommy Elwood had decided to investigate. As had Frances Nickerson and grumpy Diane, who thought that maybe Elwood's Market was on fire and wouldn't that just take the cake, after a Christmas like this!

"Oh," exclaimed Miranda when she got to the bonfire and saw Pasha's little red head sticking out of Anna's coat. Tears began to run down her cheeks as she stood there, thinking about how she hadn't really believed she would find Pasha, and how she loved Pasha, and her grandmother, and she couldn't wait to get back home to write about tonight.

Will Campbell caught the tears with his pencil and kept on drawing.

Edward Crimmins stood next to Neddie and said quietly, "This is some bonfire, isn't it."

Neddie had never seen anything so beautiful in his entire life. He looked up at his father and said, "I love this bonfire!"

Will made a few quick lines, to capture the curve of Edward Crimmins's arm on Neddie's shoulder. Then his pencil lingered a little longer, to record the light of adoration in Neddie Crimmins's eyes.

This is really most astonishing, thought Frances Nickerson. With so many people here, there is so little talking. Well, perhaps it is an improvement. Or perhaps it's simply too cold for conversation. She noticed that a window was open on the second floor of Elwood's Market. Will Campbell, she thought. That's where he lives. Oh, well, he's an artist, and artists are very absentminded.

Frances Nickerson made a note to walk this way tomorrow morning. If the window was still open, she would close it herself.

# *Chapter Fourteen*

WHENEVER PEOPLE tell the story of Ryland Falls, they always go back to the snowstorm as the big event that changed the town.

Before the snowstorm there was no Ryland Falls

Museum. Edward Crimmins had not yet donated the funds to build it. That came after Will Campbell painted *Giovanni's Bonfire.* When Edward Crimmins first laid eyes on it, he declared it was so magnificent that it had to have a proper place to hang.

Edward Crimmins was a clock manufacturer not an art critic, but he had definite opinions about things, and in years to come it would be a quiet source of pleasure to him to know that he had been ahead of the experts. In time, Will Campbell would become a well-known artist, and *Giovanni's Bonfire* was the painting that had established his confidence and his career.

Before the snowstorm, Ryland Falls was a pretty little town at the bottom of Old Rag Mountain. After the snowstorm, that did not change. But the sights and scenes familiar to all the people who lived there became familiar to many people who had never seen Ryland Falls, but knew it through Will Campbell's eyes.

An old vine slinging itself over the crook of a tree seems to be grieving in the arms of a stronger partner. A bush rigged with cobwebs in a vacant field is a bowl of light. And grumpy Diane, gazing wistfully through the window of Elwood's Market, dreaming of a lottery ticket she has yet to win, dreams for everyone.

Will Campbell's paintings reminded people of what they had forgotten, or never knew—that life can be sad and beautiful, lonely and dull, but it is never unimportant or without mystery. What Will Campbell saw encouraged other people to look long enough to see it all.

Ryland Falls now has another Christmas custom. Sometime during the holidays, Will Campbell always comes to the museum to tell the schoolchildren the story behind his most famous painting.

He is older now, with gray hair, and he doesn't use a skateboard to get around anymore. But he has the same pale eyes and ability to enchant children. They gather around his feet on the museum floor and listen as he tells them how one Christmas night he was packing to leave Ryland Falls forever when he looked out the window and saw Giovanni's bonfire—hanging behind them on the wall.

Some of the children can point to people in the

painting they know, such as Miranda Bridgeman, whose books are now in the local library, and Neddie Crimmins, who became an architect and has children of his own. Their parents recognize many of the older people gathered around the bonfire, such as Tommy Elwood and Frances Nickerson, who now rest in peace on top of Cemetery Hill. And on one particular day not so long ago, after Will had finished his usual talk, a dark-eyed young woman no one recognized walked up to him and said, "That little girl with the cat is me."

Will's eyes widened. "Anna?" Giovanni had often spoken of her, wondered how she was.

She nodded. "Sitting on my mother's lap. Only I didn't know I was sitting for my portrait, too."

Will laughed. The grown-up Anna had the same direct gaze as the little girl in the painting. She leaned forward and stared intently at her younger self.

"When I was little," she said, "I used to lie a lot. It was a way of making things come out the way I wanted. And then we moved in with my grandmother and I didn't have to tell stories anymore. But whenever I thought about that Christmas we spent in Ryland

Falls, the more I wondered how much of what I remembered was just made up."

She took her eyes off the picture and looked at Will. "Now I know that everything I remembered was true."

"As true as I could make it," Will replied.

Will's first painting of Giovanni was not his last. Over the years, Will visited him on the mountain many times. They would sit in front of the woodstove and talk about the weather or look at Lucia's book or not talk at all and just let the friendship grow in peaceful silence between them. Usually Will brought along a sketchbook. And several times a year, he brought his class.

The children loved to go to Old Rag. Giovanni would show them how he made his tools, got water out of his well, and used what he found on the floor of the forest in different ways, such as turning a tree root into a door handle, or weaving an old vine into a sturdy basket. Will would sit there quietly and draw. By the time Giovanni died, the people of Ryland Falls knew and loved the reclusive woodsman well.

But there is one figure in the painting nobody except Will Campbell remembers at all. He is standing slightly in the shadows, to one side of Giovanni. Tall and solemn, without looking sad, he gazes not upon the bonfire but upon the townspeople, as if he were silently recording who was there.

Once, the stranger raised his eyes and looked up at the window, where Will was sitting out of sight, and a smile played around his lips—as if he knew a secret or was part of a plan that nobody standing around the bonfire knew anything about.

"Who was he?" asked one of the children.

"He wasn't anybody from Ryland Falls," said Will. "But I remember thinking at the time that maybe I had passed him in the street or seen him looking out from behind a restaurant window."

"Maybe he was an angel," another child said.

Will Campbell smiled. "That's a suggestion that has been made before. I don't know. I just painted what I saw."

Every Christmas, the mystery of the stranger standing next to Giovanni is reexamined and so far no conclusion has been drawn. But before the snowstorm, very few people in Ryland Falls would have come down on the side of an angel. Now, people's imaginations seem to be more open to possibilities—about everything.

On the surface, one might not notice anything terribly different about Ryland Falls. At Christmastime, people still put electric candles in their front windows, enter the gingerbread-house contest, and attend the *Messiah* sing-along. They make lists, bake fruitcakes, and go to caroling parties. Who is going to get the tree is a question that has not entirely been resolved.

But newcomers to the town marvel at the way everyone seems to move toward Christmas as if they were being carried upon the current of a deep and reliable river. Most of the world quickens its step the closer it gets to Christmas. In Ryland Falls, the opposite is true. People become more peaceful, their steps become more measured, as if they don't want to disturb anything important that is getting ready to happen.

Or not happen.

Nobody in Ryland Falls expects history to repeat itself. But the closer it gets to Christmas, the larger is the general sense of expectation—as if the entire town stands ready to experience something extraordinary that could involve angels or the sudden descent of a mighty force that changes everything.

Like the snow.